FOR MY
SISTERS:
SHEILA
AND
ALIX

TRESPASSER ALERT

XIAN HAS LOST HER BACKPACK AND CELL IN THE FLOODING PIPES. THE FLOWING WATER WILL HELP SOMETHING ELSE LOST LONG AGO TO BE FOUND.

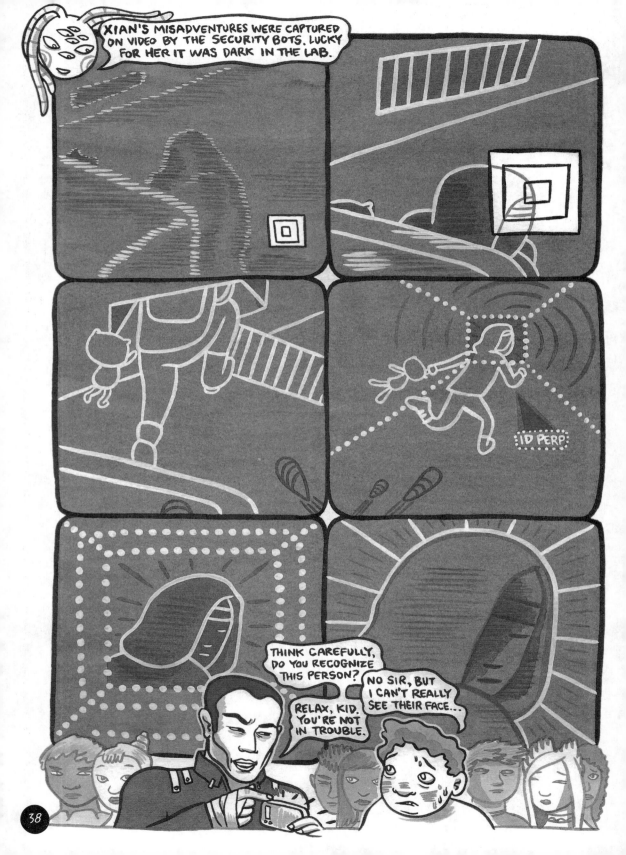

LOLY'S MECHANICAL HEART BREAKS FOR XIAN. A CHILL COMES OVER XIAN. SHE HARDENS HER OWN, HUMAN HEART A LITTLE BIT MORE THAN IT ALREADY WAS.

57

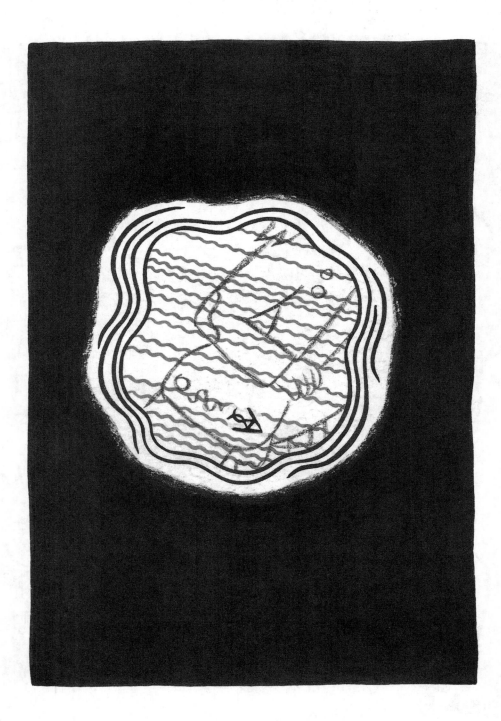

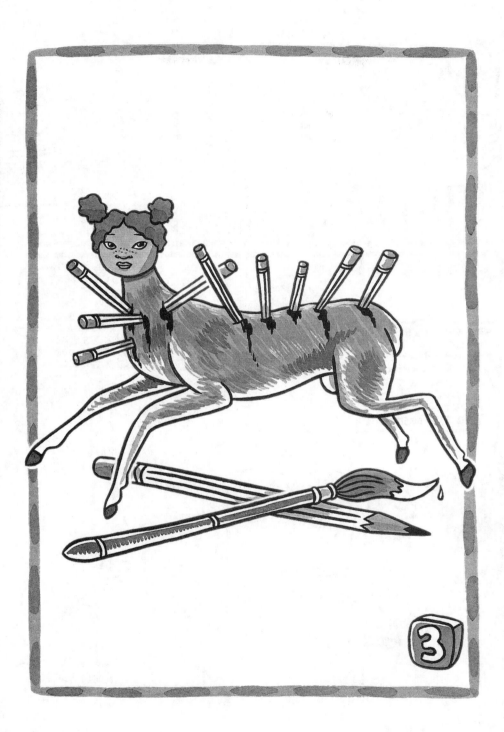

AFTER-SCHOOL ROUTINES CONTINUE AS USUAL. MIA FOCUSES ON HER JOB AT ST. ANTHONY'S, A WELCOME RESPITE FROM HER HOME LIFE.

... THEY JUST DON'T GET THAT IT'S NOT ABOUT PRETTY PICTURES, IT'S ABOUT CREATIVITY AND FREEDOM! FRIENDS CAN BE PRETTY DEAF TOO...

MIA IS AWARE FROM HER TIME AT ST. ANTHONY'S THAT MRS. C MAY BE EXPERIENCING THE EARLY STAGES OF DEMENTIA. MIA FEELS LIKE SHE'S LOSING HER FRIENDS ONE BY ONE.

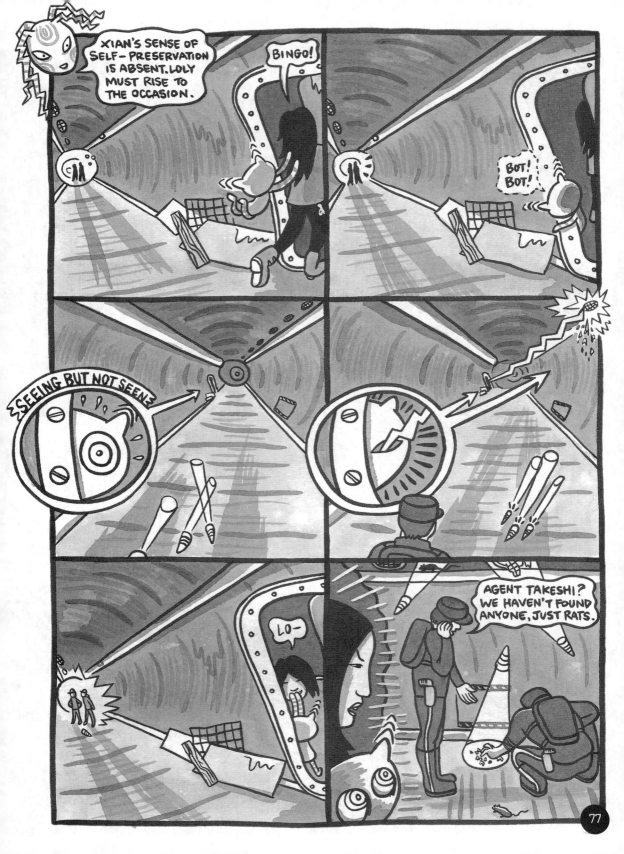

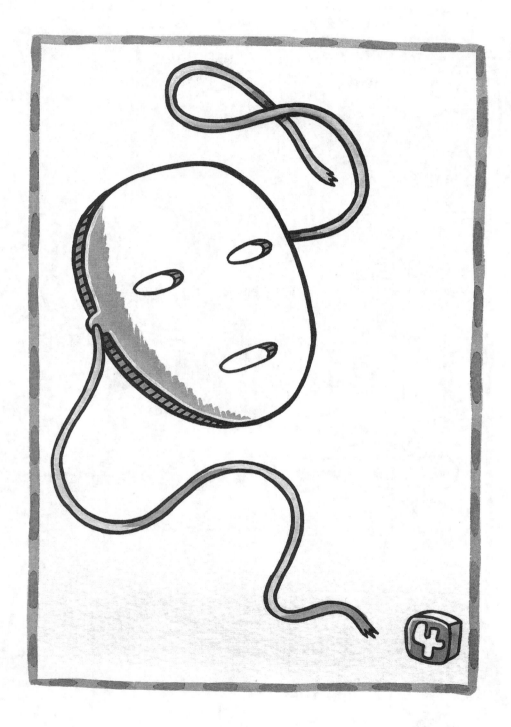

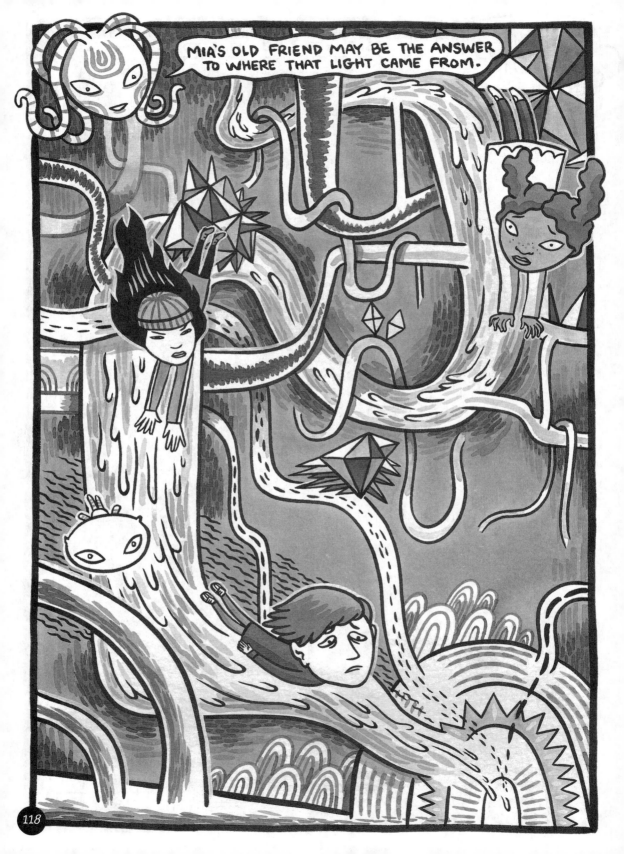

AMELIA'S TAG BECKONS THE THREE FRIENDS BACK DOWN THE RABBIT HOLE.

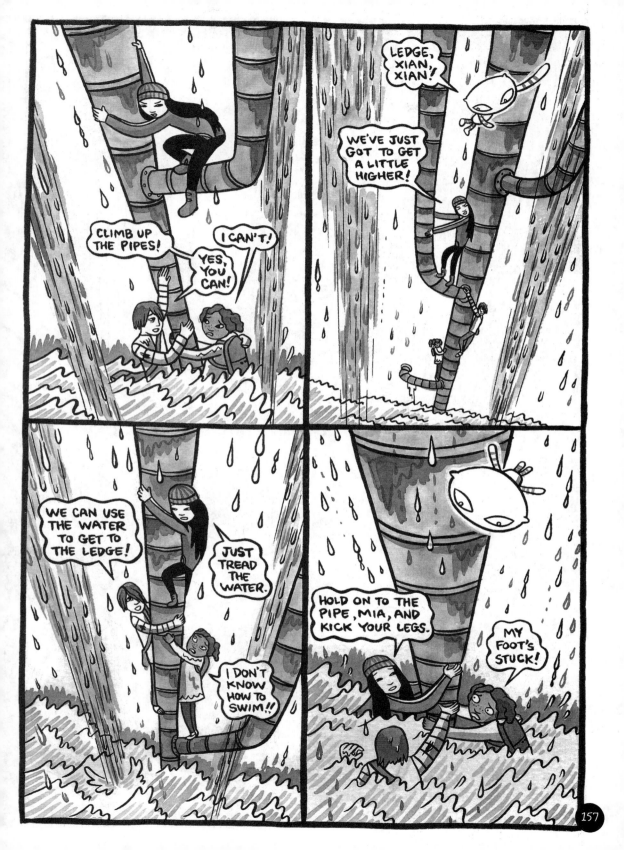

157

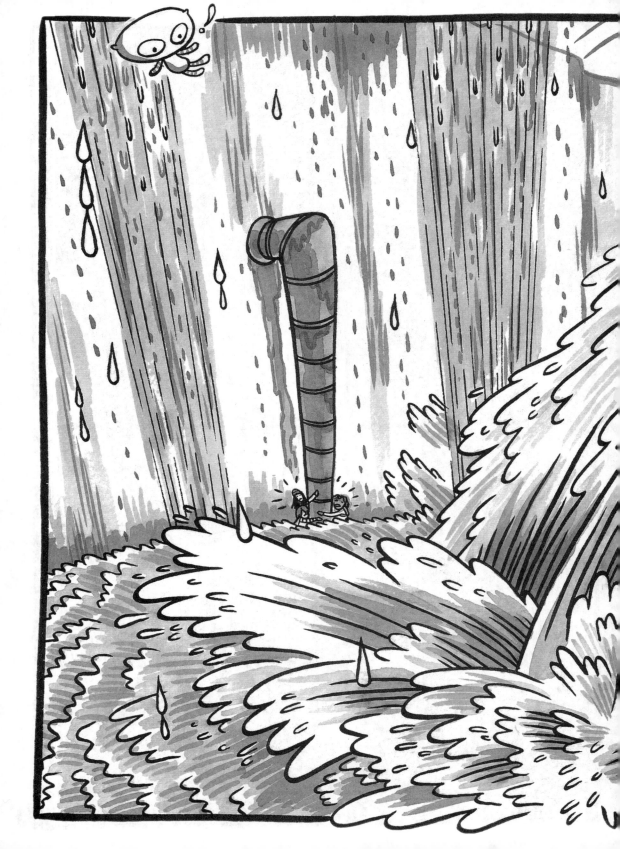

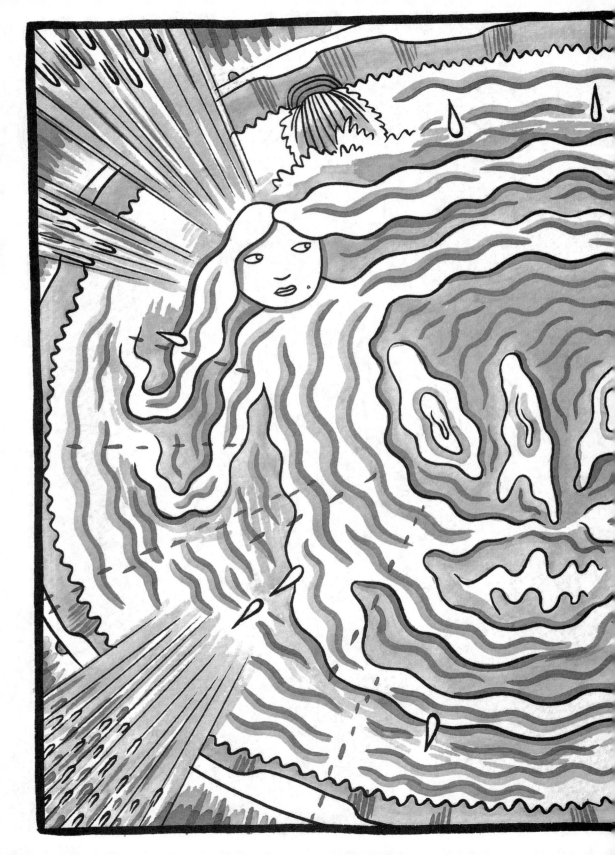

LOLY, HELP MIA FIRST!!

177

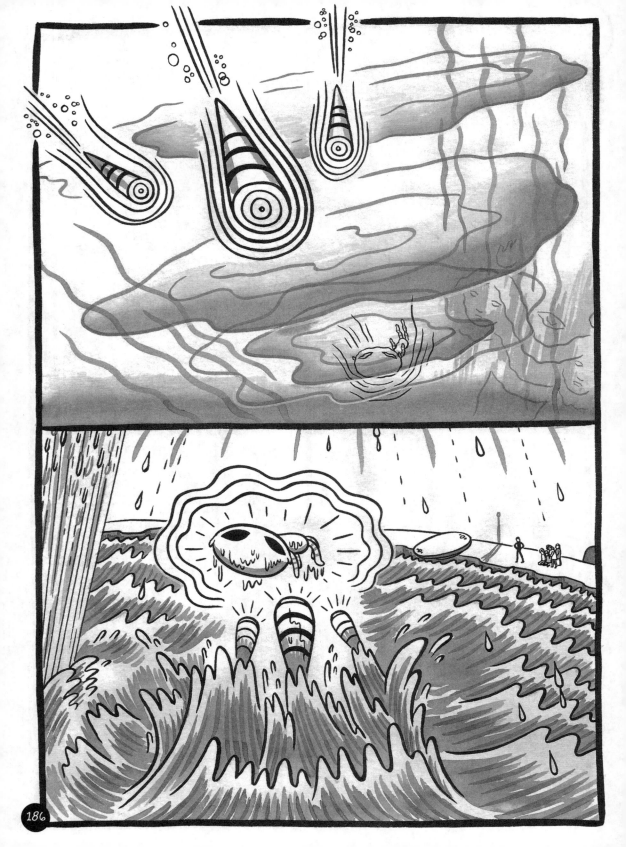

AGENT TAKESHI AND DR. DOHERTY HELP JESSE AND HIS FRIENDS ESCAPE THE TREACHEROUS BASIN. THEY TAKE REFUGE IN THE GOVERNMENT SKYLAB.

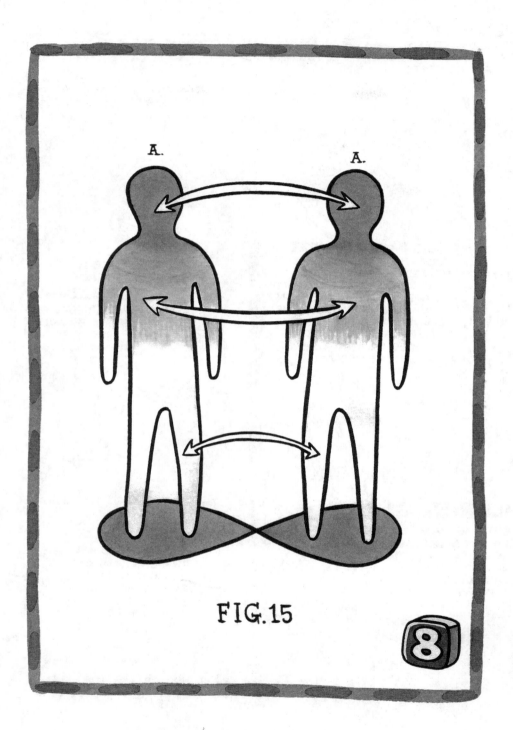

FIG. 15

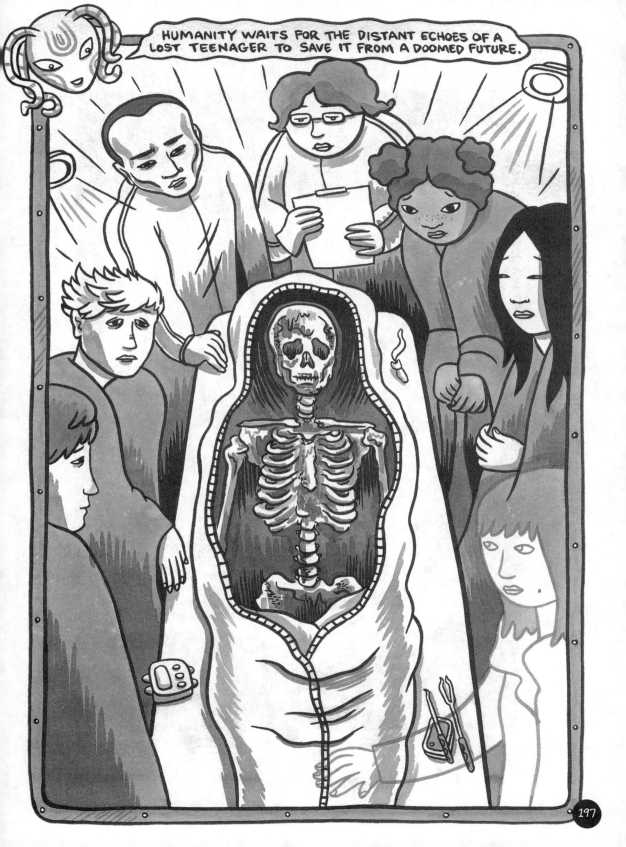

AMELIA'S WORDS TRAVEL OVER 60 YEARS' PASSAGE OF TIME.

DEAR MUM AND DAD,
I'M SORRY TO SAY GOODBYE IN A LETTER BUT I COULDN'T SAY IT IN PERSON – I MIGHT CHANGE MY MIND. YOU GUYS HAVE ALWAYS TAUGHT ME TO STAND UP FOR MY BELIEFS AND I'M DOING THAT NOW.

EVER SINCE MY DIAGNOSIS, MY ORGANS KEEP FALLING APART. WE ALL KNOW THE MULTIPLE TRANSPLANTS I NEED TO SURVIVE AREN'T GOING TO HAPPEN. RARE BLOOD TYPE, REMEMBER? DOUBLE WHAMMY, LUCKY ME.

I KNOW YOU'VE TRIED EVERYTHING TO SAVE ME.

I KNOW YOU'VE PAID A FORTUNE YOU CAN'T AFFORD FOR THIS SPECIAL CLINIC.

BUT I'VE SPENT HOURS IN THIS PLACE STARING AT THE CEILING, WAITING FOR TESTS TO START, RESULTS TO BE RETURNED. IT'S NO DIFFERENT THAN THE REGULAR HOSPITAL. I'VE HAD ENOUGH.

BUT THIS PLACE IS DIFFERENT, ISN'T IT? THERE'S A WHOLE AREA WHERE PATIENTS AREN'T ALLOWED. I FIGURED IT WAS SOME KIND OF NUCLEAR SCIENCE OR SOMETHING.

CLINIC PERSONNEL ONLY

DO NOT ENTER

IT'S REALLY AN ILLEGAL CLONE LAB!
BUT YOU GUYS KNOW THAT ALREADY, DON'T YOU?

BUT DID YOU KNOW ABOUT HER?
SHE'S JUST LIKE ME, BUT WITH SHORTER HAIR AND HEALTHY ORGANS.

YOU GUYS PROBABLY THOUGHT YOU WERE SIGNING UP FOR A
BRAIN-DEAD ORGAN BANK, THE WAY CLONES ARE SUPPOSED
TO BE. BUT SHE'S A LIVE, THINKING GIRL-LIKE ME.

WE'VE SECRETLY BECOME FRIENDS. SISTERS, REALLY.

SHE'S CHOSEN THE NAME CAMILLA BECAUSE IT'S MY MIDDLE NAME. I CALL HER CAMMIE.

I STARTED TO REALIZE THAT WE HAD MORE IN COMMON THAN I THOUGHT. I MIGHT HAVE A TERMINAL ILLNESS BUT CAMMIE HAS ANOTHER KIND OF DEATH SENTENCE HANGING OVER HER, AND IT'S BECAUSE OF ME!!

CAMMIE IS JUST DISCOVERING THIS WORLD, HER LIFE HAS JUST BEGUN. YOU GUYS TAUGHT ME TO BE A CARING PERSON, SOMEONE WHO DOES THE RIGHT THING. I KNOW YOU ARE TRYING TO SAVE YOUR ONLY CHILD BUT THERE ARE TWO OF US NOW.

I CANNOT LET YOU AND THE LAB TRADE IN CAMMIE'S LIFE FOR MINE. THESE TRANSPLANTS MIGHT NOT EVEN WORK. I'VE CREATED AN ESCAPE PLAN TO SAVE CAMMIE. MY DAYS ARE COMING TO AN END BUT HERS ARE JUST GETTING STARTED.

MY FATE IS DECIDED, BUT IF I CAN HELP CAMMIE GAIN A NEW LIFE, THEN I WILL LIVE ON IN SOME WAY.

THEY TELL ME THE TRANSPLANTS WILL TAKE PLACE THREE DAYS FROM NOW. THEY ALSO TELL ME I CAN'T VISIT YOU BECAUSE OF THE DANGER OF INFECTION.

I UNDERSTAND THAT YOU ACTED OUT OF LOVE, THAT YOU WANTED ME TO GROW OLD WITH YOU, BUT IT'S NOT GOING TO HAPPEN. IT CAN'T.

CAMMIE DESERVES TO LIVE AS MUCH AS I DO. MORE SO. I HAD MY CHANCE. HERS HAS JUST BEGUN.

I LOVE YOU BOTH DEARLY BUT I CAN'T LIVE IF IT MEANS CAMMIE HAS TO DIE. I ALWAYS WISHED FOR A SISTER, AND NOW I HAVE HER. I HOPE YOU WILL BE ABLE TO FORGIVE MY DECISION.

LOVE ALWAYS, AMELIA

THE ESCAPE WAS EASY. I PLANNED WELL, NO ONE SAW US.

I'VE BROUGHT SURVIVAL STUFF. WE NEED TO STAY UNDERGROUND FOR AT LEAST A WEEK.

WE'VE RUN OUT OF FOOD AND WATER. CAMMIE HAS TO GO ABOVE GROUND. SHE'S NEVER BEEN OUTSIDE BEFORE, BUT I'M TOO WEAK TO GO.

I'VE GOT TO TRUST THAT SHE CAN HANDLE IT.

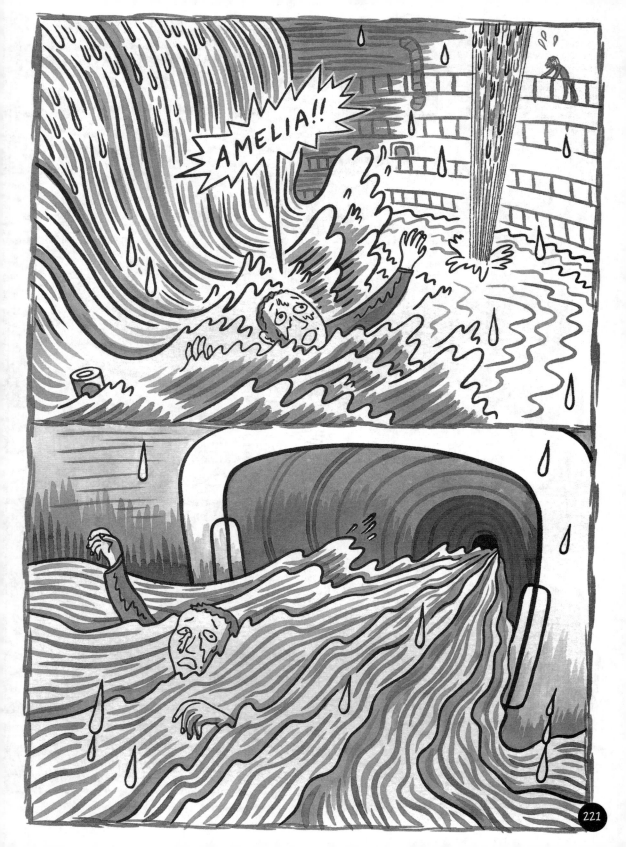

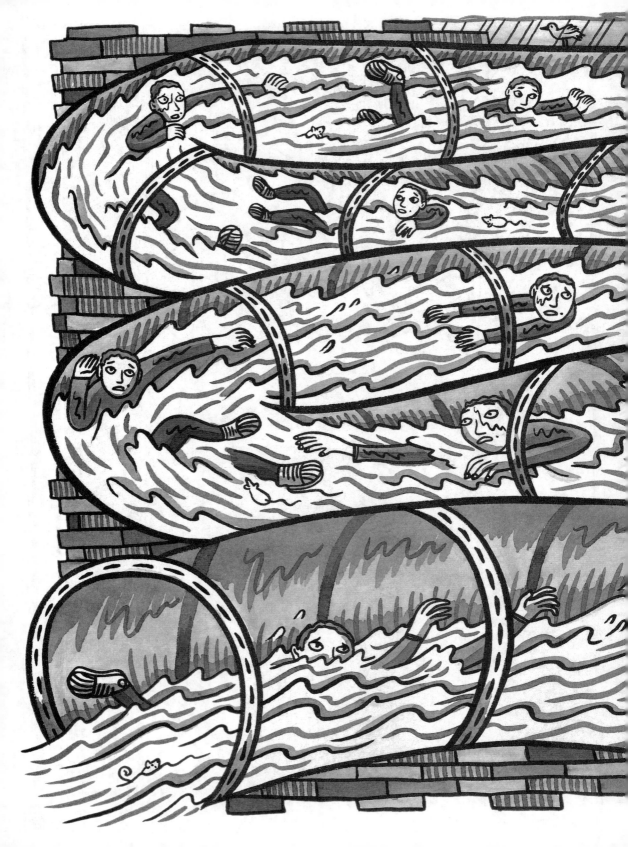

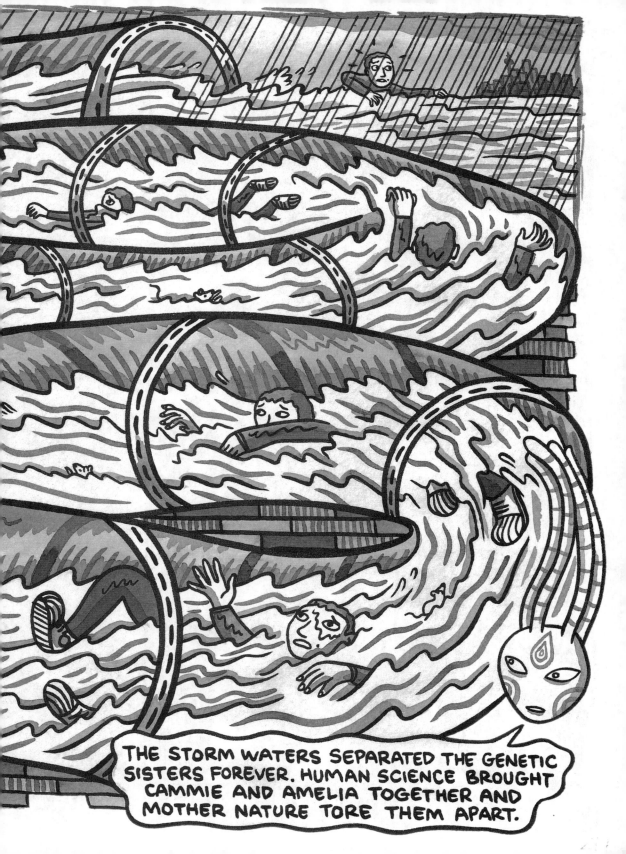

229

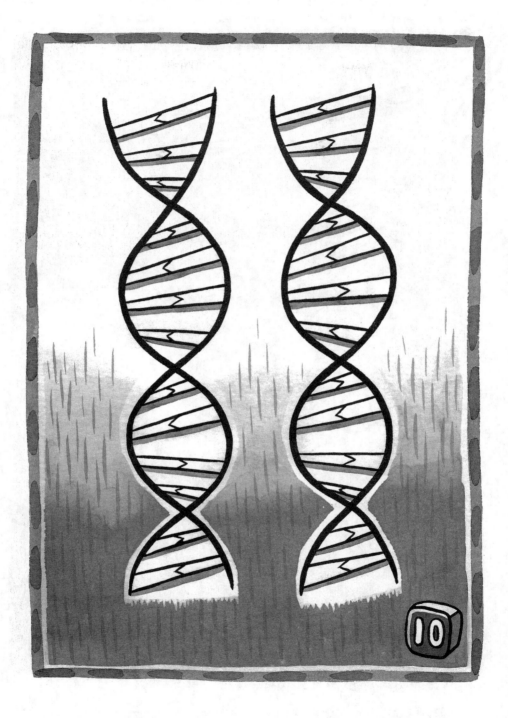

ACKNOWLEDGMENTS

THANK YOU TO THE ONTARIO ARTS COUNCIL'S WRITERS' RESERVE GRANT FOR GENEROUS SUPPORT IN THE CREATION OF THIS BOOK.

MANY THANKS TO THE ANNICK PRESS CREW: TO SHERYL SHAPIRO FOR INITIATING TNW, TO KATIE HEARN FOR GREAT PATIENCE, AND ESPECIALLY TO DAVID WICHMAN, EDITOR EXTRAORDINAIRE, FOR INSIGHT AND CREATIVITY THAT TRANSFORMED TNW INTO AN EPIC TALE!

THANKS EVER AND ALWAYS TO CRAIG DANIELS FOR UNWAVERING LOVE AND SUPPORT THESE MANY YEARS.

FIONA SMYTH IS A CARTOONIST, PAINTER, AND ILLUSTRATOR.
SHE GREW UP IN MONTREAL READING ASTERIX AND OBELIX,
MAD MAGAZINE, AND THE ENGLISH CARTOONIST GILES.
HER PREVIOUS COMICS WORK HAS INCLUDED LONG-RUNNING
STRIPS IN *EXCLAIM!* MAGAZINE, *VICE*, AND FOUR ISSUES OF
THE VORTEX COMIC BOOK *NOCTURNAL EMISSIONS*. A COLLECTION
OF HER *EXCLAIM!* STRIPS WAS PUBLISHED AS *CHEEZ 100* BY
PEDLAR PRESS IN 2001. SHE WAS A CONTRIBUTOR TO THE
SECOND VOLUME OF *TWISTED SISTERS*.
FIONA'S ILLUSTRATIONS WERE USED IN NICKELODEON'S
THE BIG HELP VOLUNTEERISM CAMPAIGN.

FIONA CITES FRANK HERBERT'S *DUNE* AS ONE OF HER
FAVORITE BOOKS. HER FAVORITE GRAPHIC NOVELS INCLUDE
SKIBBER BEE BYE, *SKIM*, *PERSEPOLIS*, AND *WHAT IT IS*.
SHE IS AN AVID ZINESTER AND COLLECTOR OF ZINES.

FIONA IS CURRENTLY TEACHING AT OCADU
(ONTARIO COLLEGE OF ART & DESIGN UNIVERSITY)
AND LIVES IN TORONTO WITH HER PARTNER,
MUSICIAN CRAIG DANIELS.
THE NEVER WERES IS FIONA'S FIRST GRAPHIC NOVEL.